The
LITTLE WITCH
and the
RIDDLE

Bruce Degen

An I Can Read Book®

A Harper Trophy Book

HARPER & ROW, PUBLISHERS

*To E.E.— This story became
a Princess, a Frog, and finally a book;
with thanks for the work and the magic*

The Little Witch and the Riddle
Copyright © 1980 by Bruce Degen
All rights reserved. No part of this book may be
used or reproduced in any manner whatsoever without
written permission except in the case of brief quotations
embodied in critical articles and reviews. Printed in
the United States of America. For information address
Harper & Row, Junior Books, 10 East 53rd Street,
New York, N.Y. 10022. Published simultaneously in
Canada by Fitzhenry & Whiteside Limited, Toronto.

Library of Congress Cataloging in Publication Data
Degen. Bruce.
    The little witch and the riddle.

    (An I can read book)
    SUMMARY: A little witch and her friend Otto
Ogre must find the answers to the riddle before
they can open the book of magic secrets.
    [1. Witches—Fiction.   2. Friendship—Fiction]
I. Title.
PZ7.D3635Li   [E]   78-19475
ISBN 0-06-021414-7
ISBN 0-06-021415-5 (lib. bdg.)
ISBN 0-06-444125-3 (pbk.)

First Harper Trophy edition, 1988.

Contents

1. A Magic Gift

Lily was a little witch.
She knew a little magic
and she made big pots
of Witch's Brew.

Otto Ogre liked to help.

He brought the wood

for the fire.

One day Otto asked,

"Can I mix the Witch's Brew?"

"No," said Lily. "This is magic.

Witches know about magic,

but ogres do not."

"I could learn," said Otto.

"Humph!" said Lily.

They heard a knock at the door.

"Who is it?" called Lily.

"Big package for a little witch,"

said the goblin who was carrying it.

Lily opened the package

and pulled out a big book.

"The Magic Secrets

of Grandmother Witch!" she cried.

"Wow! Now I can learn

to fly on my broomstick."

"Me too?" asked Otto softly.

"Magic is only for witches,"

said Lily.

But there was a big lock

on the book.

"Where is the key?" asked Lily.

She looked in the box

but there was no key.

"I will use magic

to open the lock," said Lily.

"OPEN SESAME," she shouted.

The book did not open.

"HOCUS POCUS," she yelled.

Still the book did not open.

13

Lily got a big hammer.

"I will smash the lock," she said.

"Is *that* magic?" asked Otto.

"Wait!" cried the goblin.

"I almost forgot to give you

this riddle.

The book will open

when you solve it."

Lily read the riddle:

Find a Handful
of Laughter,
Find a Handful
of Tears,
Then a Helping Hand
Leads
To What Everyone
Needs.

have fun! from Grandma.

"What is this?" cried Lily.

"What is a Handful of Laughter?

And what is a Handful of Tears?

And what does Everyone Need?"

17

"I do not know the answers,"

said the goblin.

"My job was only to bring the riddle.

It was not my job to understand it."

The goblin flew away.

"I do not understand

this riddle either,"

Lily said sadly.

"So how will I ever find the answers?

And how will I ever read

my grandmother's magic book?"

She began to cry.

"Do not cry," said Otto.

"I will help you.

We will go out

and look for the answers."

Otto and Lily put on their boots
and mufflers and mittens.
Then they started out
to look for the answers
to the riddle.

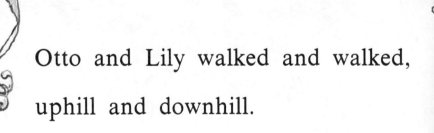

2. A Handful of Laughter

Otto and Lily walked and walked, uphill and downhill.

They came to a lake.

"I hear something," said Otto.

"Honk! Honk! Honk!"

cried Goose.

"What is the matter, Goose?"

asked Otto.

"My foot is caught

in this fishing line,"

said Goose.

"I cannot fly. Help me!"

"We are too busy," said Lily.

"Hurry, Otto."

"Wait," said Otto.

"It will only take a minute."

25

He pulled the fishing line this way.

He pulled the fishing line that way.

The knot came out.

26

"Ah!" said Goose. "That is better."

"Can you help us too?"

asked Otto.

He read the riddle to Goose.

"Find a Handful of Laughter.

Find a Handful of Tears.

Then a helping hand leads

to What Everyone Needs.

Do you know where to find

a Handful of Laughter?"

asked Otto.

"No," said Goose. "But I know
the last part of the riddle.
I know What Everyone Needs:
Feathers!
Feathers keep you warm.
Feathers keep you dry.
Without feathers you cannot fly."

Goose gave Otto one of her feathers.

"Maybe this will help you," she said.

"Now winter is coming.

I must fly south. Good-by."

"A feather," said Lily.

"That is silly."

Otto looked at the feather.

He scratched his ear with it.

It made him smile.

Suddenly he tickled Lily.

"Ha ha, ho ho, hee hee!" she laughed.

Otto shouted,

"Here is your Handful of Laughter."

"Otto!" said Lily. "You have answered the first part of the riddle.

You are very clever."

3. A Handful of Tears

Otto and Lily walked on and on.

They crossed a meadow.

They heard someone crying,

"Oh my, oh my, oh my!"

It was Mole.

He was walking in a circle.

He bumped into Otto.

"Help," cried Mole.

"I lost my glasses.

I cannot see a thing.

Will you help me find them?"

"Sorry," said Lily.

"We must hurry."

"Wait," said Otto.

"We can look

for his glasses."

35

Otto looked up

and Otto looked down.

At last he saw a spiderweb.

There was something shiny

caught in it…Mole's glasses.

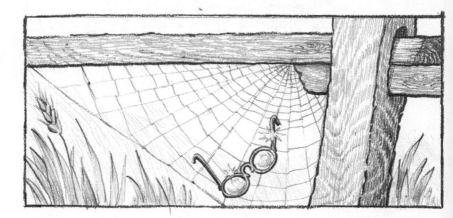

Otto wiped the glasses

and gave them to Mole.

"Thanks," said Mole

as he put on his glasses.

"I can see again."

Otto asked, "Can you help us too?"

He showed the riddle to Mole.

Mole read:

"Find a Handful of Laughter.

Find a Handful of Tears.

Then a helping hand leads

to What Everyone Needs."

Otto asked,

"Do you know where to find

a Handful of Tears?"

"No," said Mole, "but I do know

the last part of the riddle.

I know What Everyone Needs:

Food! A full pantry!

Winter is coming.

When snow covers the ground,

everyone needs a deep burrow

full of roots to eat."

Mole went down into his burrow.

"Here is a nice big onion for you,"
he said. "I hope you enjoy it.
And now, good-by."

"An onion!" said Lily. "How silly."

"Let me think," said Otto.

He looked at the onion.

He sniffed the onion.

He took out his pocketknife
and cut the onion in half.

Suddenly Otto put the onion
under Lily's nose.

"Don't!" yelled Lily.

"It makes me cry."

"Yes," Otto shouted.

"Here is your Handful of Tears."

43

Lily was surprised.

"You found another answer!

You are *very* clever.

Otto, my clever friend.

Let's hurry and solve the riddle."

44

They walked on and on.

Snow began to fall.

"I am cold," said Lily.

"We must go home," said Otto.

"But we have not found

the last answer to the riddle,"

said Lily.

"If it keeps snowing," said Otto,

"we will not find the way home."

The snow fell faster.

"I cannot see!" cried Lily.

"I cannot walk anymore."

"Hold my hand," said Otto.

They walked slowly in the snow.

Finally Otto saw something.

"Look over there," he said.

"Home!" cried Lily. "We are home!"

4. What Everyone Needs

Lily and Otto

took off their hats and mittens

and mufflers and boots.

Lily put them by the fire to dry.

Then Lily read the riddle again.

"Find a Handful of Laughter.

Find a Handful of Tears.

Then a helping hand leads

to What Everyone Needs.

Otto, you found

the Handful of Laughter.

And you found

the Handful of Tears.

But where is the helping hand

that leads to What Everyone Needs?"

Lily thought and thought.

"Otto!" she cried suddenly.

"Goose needed you,

Mole needed you,

and I needed you.

You are the answer to the riddle!"

"Me?" asked Otto.

"You are the helping hand," said Lily.

"And you are What Everyone Needs:

a true friend!"

Lily hugged Otto.

Suddenly the book opened.

"Look!" cried Otto.

"We solved the riddle," said Lily.

"That proves it!"

Lily picked up the book
to get ready for magic.
Otto picked up his boots
to get ready to leave.

"Otto, my friend," said Lily,

"this snow will last a long time.

Will you stay

and read my magic book with me?"

"Great Jumping Goblins!"

shouted Otto.

"Of course!"

So Lily and Otto began to read
the magic book.

"Here is a magic spell for me,"
cried Otto.

"HOAKUS CROAKUS!"

And Otto changed into a frog.

"And here is a spell for me,"

said Lily.

"ALACAZEE!

DON'T SEE ME!"

Lily disappeared.

"Come back!" cried Otto.

"And here is the spell

to change us back," said Lily.

"ALACAZAM!

MAGIC SCRAM!"

Now Otto and Lily were

Otto and Lily again.

"But here is the best spell of all,"

said Lily. "Say it with me, Otto."

They shouted together,

"SHA–BOOM!

FLY BROOM!"

Lily's broom began to float.

Lily and Otto climbed on.

Then Lily and Otto flew off

over the snow

and under the moon.

"Magic is best with friends,"

said Lily.